Y0-BPZ-688

As the Mountain Moved

Hedwig Andrae

A Story of Switzerland

Published by
L& E Family Books
4186 Hwy T
Shelbyville, MO. 63469
573.633.1019

As The Mountain Moved
First printed in 1891. Taken from 1907 printing

Scripture quotes from King James Version

ISBN 0-9774975-7-7

968668

Introduction

AS THE MOUNTAIN MOVED is a touching story of how at least six people found salvation and peace in Jesus through reading of the New Testament, which they had been forbidden to do.

The catastrophe mentioned in this book took place in the early 1800's. The mountains, places, and villages mentioned can be found today in Switzerland. We have no way of knowing if everything mentioned happened, but it is possible.

The setting is in the mountains of Switzerland in 1805 and 1806 with people who were very loyal to the Catholic church.

•Berena, a maiden of 17, whose mother had died when she was very young.
•Berena's troubled father, Franz Wendelin.
•Lorenz Waser and his two younger brothers, Ulrich, 12 and Matthew, 10, sons of a rich farmer.
•Josepha, whose father seemingly had been murdered a few years earlier.
•An old fisherman, Michael Engler, living alone on a small island in the Lowerzer Sea by the mountains.

Acknowledgments

A Special Thanks to:

Myron Hostetler, for sharing the book, *Als Der Berg Wanderte.*

Laurence Kropf, for translating the book from German to English.

Carolyn Bürgi, for sharing photos of the area that are used on the cover and in the book. Also for the old postcard from Switzerland.

Arlyn Hostetler, cover design.

Mary Hostetler, editing.

Pauline Knox, proofreading.

Publisher's Note

This book was first published in Switzerland in the German language. In the course of time it traveled across the ocean to western Colorado, where it was placed in a box of books at a garage sale. This box of books was purchased by Myron Hostetler. From there the book found its way to the Midwest where it was translated into English. It is now a compelling storybook.

The publishers have made slight changes and adaptions for clarity, and to make it more suitable for readers in the plain communities.

The front cover pictures the mountains Rossberg and Rigi as they appear today. A postcard drawing of how it was before the mountain-slide is on pages 2 and 113.

Index

As the Mountain Moved

Chapter 1

In wondrous beauty the Lowerzer Sea rests between the mountains of Switzerland. In the still, clear waters are mirrored green forests and blue heavens. Golden sunshine sparkles on the barely stirred waters and the two mountains, Rigi and Rossberg, send their greeting over the lovely villages of Lowerz and Goldau to the quiet sea.

Rigi and Rossberg, what weird companions! Now they look down restful and peaceful, but how much calamity have they in store for the golden meadow? How much destruction may still be slumbering under the high towering steep precipice mass of the deceiving Rossberg, "The Rufiberg" as the people called the famed colossal rock?

"I don't trust him, the old Rufiberg," said the young man as with powerful oar strokes he parted the light waves of the sea. His boat companions, two boys of ten and twelve years, and a blooming young girl who just now seemed to have outgrown her childish shoes, listened with interest.

The young girl directed her dark questioning eyes somewhat anxiously, first to the speaker and then to the wild precipice rock formations of the defamed Rufiberg, her own beloved mountain which from childhood she had considered as her home, for this was truly her home. Did not her father's house, the wonderful beloved Spitzibühl stand in-between the soft green meadows of the Rufiberg?

The eyes of the maiden hung full of love, almost honor, to the clean built-up farmstead that with white walls and red roofs, so fresh and inviting, was to be seen peeping out of the surrounding trees and green meadows. How she loved each corner and peak of her childhood home, indeed her whole mountain.

She looked up higher. Above the Spitzibühl were the forests; first deciduous trees, then fir trees, larch, and pine. Still higher and more scattered, all the way up, were low scrub trees. Above this, barren and rocky, towering to the sky, stood the Wildespitz with the iron cross on it.

She could not see the cross from the boat since it was too far away, but she knew it was there. She had been there many times and had sat on the stone at the foot of the cross, dreamily looking down on her beloved valley, the blooming garden and the golden meadow.

"No, no, it cannot be evil, my old Rufiberg," she said, shaking her head and almost questioningly looking into the brown eyes of the young man, who had been watching her all this time. "Is it not true, Lorenz, that we need not be afraid of him?"

He laughed out loud. "Fear?! No true Swiss needs to fear, and also no Swiss girl." Nodding he added, "But that the old Rossberg has in the past brought about many distressing things stands undeniable, though it be hundreds of years ago. Sometimes the mountain is overcome with the desire to wander," he added mysteriously.

The two boys now scooted closer. They were brothers. This could be seen at first glance. The same dark brown full hair, the flashing blue eyes, full of life and interest, also the same defiant forehead and the energetic mouth. They were at the age when a person likes to hear of happenings. Especially Ulrich, who at twelve years old greatly desired to hear of any kind of adventurous or remarkable experience. He laid his robust brown hand on his brother's oar and spoke excitedly, "Tell us, Lorenz, tell us! How was it that the Rossberg wandered?"

Lorenz shook off his hand and said, "Let loose, Ulrich, we must go forward, otherwise we won't get our fishes. You know also that I can't tell you about that. Old Michael Engler can do that. You know I wasn't there when the mountain moved. Just wait till we experience it ourselves."

"Oh Lorenz, don't say so!" cried Berena. "We may not experience it ever. We live so wonderfully peaceful and secure." Again she glanced back to her mountain. It looked so firm and trustworthy.

"You keep on trusting," said Lorenz soothingly. "Today and tomorrow it will not move, and further into the future your little head need not worry about it."

"There is the island Schwanau!" called Matthew, the youngest, waving his woolen hat. "Greet God, Michael Engler!"

Like two little ornamental boxes, the two islands, Schwanau and Lutzeau became visible out of the clear blue waters of the Lowerzer. The nicest indeed was the Schwanau, with its weather-beaten castle ruins, the little chapel and the little fish house. They lay there like a picture mirrored by the playing waves, overlooked far in the background by the towering mountain range with its snow-covered peaks.

On the other side rose Drusberg, Silbern and Ortstock, the majestic Uri-Ortstock with its perpetual snow-cap. Above all toward heaven, stood towering gigantic rock pyramids which became completely devoid of all their tree ornaments through a fourteen-day fearful forest fire in August of 1800. They now towered into the air, naked and barren and fully isolated.

Quiet and peaceful the Schwanau let itself be looked on by the gigantic mountains. On its shore stood the fisher, Michael Engler, ready to receive his guests.

He had an extremely attractive form, wearing the same leather pants and brown wool jacket as his younger friend, Lorenz Waser and his brothers were wearing. His honorable head was covered with thick white hair and on his friendly face rested a peace which could not come from his beautiful surroundings alone.

"This peace comes from the inside out," thought Lorenz Waser many times, the rich farmer's son from the Schwendi-Alp at the Rigi. For being often with the old man, his sharp eyes observed that Michael's peace was not conditional on his surroundings or condition, but that it remained the same in the worst conditions, in storms and bad weather. A love, strange to himself, burned in Lorenz's heart for the old man. More than that, an almost wonderful trust.

"Greet God, Lorenz," called the old man joyfully from the shore. "I have been waiting for you. Josepha from the mill was here and left a message for you. Who have you brought with you?" he added heartily while he stretched out his hand to help the young maid from the boat to the shore. "Is this not Berena Wendelin from the farm called Spitzibühl?"

"Yes, Michael, this is Berena," answered Lorenz. "I brought her along because her mother also needs Rotheli (a fish) like mine does. Do you have enough for us all?"

"Enough for all, yes indeed, also for Josepha from the mill, if you want to take them to her, Lorenz. She was here and asked for them but didn't have time to wait till I catch them. She thought you would go by the mill anyhow when you climb up the Schwendi-Alp."

A cloud came over Lorenz's forehead, but only for a moment. The evening was too nice to be pouting and when the two little boys rejoiced, saying, 'We go to the mill, there we always get something good,' he agreed to take Josepha the desired trout.

"And now Michael," said he while he chained the boat, "show us your beautiful Schwanau. Berena hasn't seen it yet and you are so proud of it you will surely gladly show it."

"And then relate to us of the Rossberg, when it moved," added Matthew.

Ulrich added excitedly, "And of the Virgin Gemma who dived into the sea. Also of the evil knight of the castle and the good Staffacher."

"That is a lot for one time," smiled the old fisher. "And children, there are so many nicer things to relate."

"True happenings?" asked the boys. "Such as

the moving mountain and the Virgin Gemma?" Their cheeks glowed and they barely had patience enough to see the island. And yet it was so beautiful, the quiet Schwanau.

Berena was in a worshipful mood as she knelt in the small chapel on the island. Her glance wandered from the quiet joyful face of the old fisherman to the image over the altar, which was different from her colorfully adorned chapel in Goldau. It was not the Virgin Mary, but the Redeemer on the cross.

Her usual prayer to Mary hesitated to come over her lips. Could this little church maybe be dedicated to the Savior? But she could not think of a prayer to Jesus and she found no words of her own. So she remained quiet, brought forth the rosary and bowed her brown head.

"How is then your church?" asked Matthew of the old fisherman as they went out. "There is not a single mother god in there. Do you then not need to pray?"

The old fisherman smiled a sad smile. "Does prayer depend on the image of Mary?" said he more to himself than to the child. "Sad, sad, would be our condition then. You can pray to God yourself, son, and besides this you need no mother god image, not even a chapel."

Frightened, Lorenz laid his finger on his mouth. “Quiet, Michael, quiet, don’t speak such blasphemy. What if the priest should hear that?”

“I am not afraid,” smiled the old man. “He doesn’t come here. Only once in a while one of the Capuchin monk brothers comes from Rigi-Klosterli the same as they come to you in Goldau. But he is always in a hurry and does not look around or say much. It is too secluded here on the Schwanau.”

“Was it formerly otherwise before Staffacher destroyed the master castle?” asked Lorenz while they were walking through the old fallen ruins.

“Yes indeed, then it was different,” nodded the old man. “Then things went in high fashion and disorderly besides. We had evil castle lords on the Schwanau.”

“Yes, yes, Berena,” added Ulrich, “and one of the knights was so evil and base that he ravished a wonderfully beautiful young virgin. Gemma was her name and because she could not escape from the island, she plunged herself into the sea.” Ulrich loved nothing better than to relate such strange happenings. His cheeks glowed and his eyes flashed.

“Listen, Ulrich,” said the old Engler now. “If you so much love the old knight stories you should choose noble knights and not evil ones.”

"Siegfried and Hartmut?" asked the boy.

"There are more noble ones," said the old fisher.

"Lately I read a book," said Lorenz. "Plazidus in the Rigi-Klosterli gave it to me. It is called *The Song of the Savior*. The knight goes through the land with twelve of His brave men. He helped the destitute, healed the sick, preached to the sorrowful the glad message from God, and fed the hungry. That is a noble good knight, Master Michael."

The old man took off his hat from his white hair. "That is Jesus of Nazareth," said he solemnly.

Berena's eyes became ever bigger. "Jesus which the Bible tells about?" she asked.

"The same," nodded Engler. "He was not only a knight, but a King, God's Son. But he lived and did what the song said, and more than that, He gave His life for us."

Ulrich listened intently. "Were we then sentenced to die?" asked he. "What have we transgressed?"

"Transgressed? Think again, son, whether you haven't done much in your life that was evil and not right. For all this evil has God sentenced you to die."

"God?" asked Ulrich incredulously.

"Yes, God! For He it is whom you grieve with

your sins, but because He loves you and does not want to see you die, He sent His son Jesus. He died in your place."

"How good of Him!" said Ulrich. "Tell us more of Him, Michael."

Then the old man related. He knew his Bible well, for here on the solitary island he could read unmolested, no priest hindered him, and neither had any until now, discovered the forbidden book in his hands.

So they sat together at the foot of the old castle ruins; the old man, the three brothers, and the young maiden. They looked on Rigi and Rossberg with their rugged rock formations and the lovely town of Goldau in the valley. They saw the white clouds moving and the water waves playing around the quiet island.

With open ears, the four youth listened to the wonderful, beautiful story of Jesus, the Saviour of the world. To Berena it seemed she had never in her life heard anything so precious. "If only this glorious Man would still live!" she thought again and again while listening to the story. The tears ran down her cheeks as she heard how he died in pain on the cross.

"Yes, yes," said Michael as he saw the tears. "That was a bitter death and for you, Berena, and for me. He has suffered so that we may be delivered. That is indeed worth crying about. Don't forget what good He has done for you."

The sun had already laid her bright beams over the waters. It was becoming late because of the story.

"You must go home," said the old fisherman, rising. "From here to the Schwendi-Alp is far, and also to the Spitzibühl it is not a short cat-spring. Come again when you want to. I look forward to seeing you."

He carefully packed each ones Rotheli in the basket and soon the boat glided quietly through the evening golden waves.

Chapter Two

The four youngsters were very quiet as they journeyed on. Little Matthew, for he was from babyhood only a tender child, and the other three had many things to think about. The words and demeanor of the old Fisherman had made a deep impression on each of them.

Silently they boated together through the small Lowerzer Sea. As they parted ways at Goldau there came only a heart-felt, “God protect you,” over their lips.

Berena turned her feet toward the fresh green Rossberg. Her beloved Spitzibühl, her home, beckoned her. The three brothers climbed up the Rigi Mountain along the bubbling creek. Soon they heard the roaring of the wild mill dam.

"Hurray! Now we go to see Josepha," called out Matthew who by this prospect became completely alive again. "Let us go to her, Lorenz."

But his big brother thought otherwise. He had no desire to greet the owner of the mill who the younger boys so much desired to see. He beckoned to the servant who took care of the place, to come. But then he was called by name.

"Lorenz Waser! Greet God!" rang out a clear maiden voice from the house. Lorenz turned around. There on the threshold she stood, the one whom he would rather not have seen.

Josepha Gurliman, the rich daughter from the mill, was the same age as Berena Wendelin from the Spitzibühl. But as Berena seemed almost as a child in form, words and demeanor, Josepha was a full-grown mature maiden who had the stamp of self-confidence and determination. Just so clearly had Berena the stamp of childlikeness and dependency.

Josepha was very beautiful, grown big and strong, like the strong fir trees of the mountains. Her face shone snow-white and her lips rose-red like the snow flower in March. With her blond hair wound in a bun at the back of her neck, the blue eyes flashing in inward passion and desires, her whole demeanor was as a queen.

Also, her dress was in accordance with her bearing. From the heavy silver hair-pins and ornamental necklace to the glittering snaps of her fancy shoes, it almost appeared as though she had so adorned herself for a special reason or occasion. Her pale blue dress and black velvet corset didn't fit for the usual work of a Saturday evening.

Lorenz noticed this and his heart began to beat a little faster. He was a little disturbed with all this, and therefore the tone of his voice was a little more harsh than he had intended as he opened the basket, saying, "Good evening, Josepha, here we have the fish you ordered from Michael Engler." He intended to unload and move on but the maiden had noticed his tone of voice.

"So curt, Lorenz," she laughed. "The youngsters must first have their apple and a piece of cake. While we go get it, rest yourself a little at the dam. Resting is good at the roaring waters."

She took the boys by the hand and went into the house with them. Lorenz remained alone at the dam and stared into the rushing waters, thinking. His thoughts went back to the old man, Engler, and to what he had said.

Could all that be true? Why was it not told to him in school? No, he could not believe it, he did not want to. Why should someone else die for his sins? He hadn't even committed any sins.

Lorenz tried hard to shake off these thoughts and to bring back into his remembrance the form of Berena in their stead.

Very dear came her form before his mind's eye. She was as a child; so simple, so innocent and so completely ignorant. In his mind he had to compare her with Josepha. Josepha was in beauty, wisdom and riches far ahead of Berena. Nor could he deny, that she held captive a piece of Lorenz Waser's heart.

They had known each other for a long time, from childhood on. Their fathers had been friends and the way from the Schwendi-Alp toward Goldau always went by the mill. Thus the children were often together and nobody had ever thought otherwise than that Josepha and Lorenz, with Schwendi-Alp and Aabach mill, would someday completely come together.

But in the last while a slight change had been taking place in Lorenz' heart. A change which became especially noticeable after he had been around Berena Wendelin. In school he had always overlooked her as a small, helpless, and fearful girl. Compared with the self-confident, able and strong millers' daughter, she didn't stand up.

Then when the quiet mother at Spitzibühl died, Berena was sent for some time to Zurich to stay with her grandmother. Her older sister, Regina, who now took the responsibility to keep house, had more than she could do to take care of all the children. Now that Berena was grown and home again she was able to help her sister take care of the little ones.

Every time Lorenz looked into her brown eyes he thought, "She, I could love." And now he thought so again.

While he looked into the rushing water it seemed to him that those brown eyes were looking back at him, and they had that questioning, seeking and anxious expression which he had seen that afternoon. He would gladly have set her at ease and comforted her.

Suddenly there appeared in the waves another image, another maiden face and a bright voice teasingly asking, "Who are you smiling about, Lorenz, yourself or me? See, the waters shove us together."

It was so. Lorenz saw it by looking up. He quickly stepped back from the bank and sat down on the grass.

"How is business going?" he asked for lack of something else to say.

Josepha drew her eyes together. She was not

interested in conversing with Lorenz about business.

Since two years ago when her father had died in a mysterious way, and soon after her mother had died of grief, she was the sole owner of the mill. Her uncle took care of the mill business, and she did not concern herself about it.

With Lorenz she gladly conversed about other things. She sat beside him on the grass and began to ask him questions. She wanted to know about his visit to the Schwanau. He related only hesitantly and rather unwillingly, for he didn't want to talk about Berena or of what Michael had told them. He had the vague impression that it might be too pure and holy to discuss it with her.

Josepha perceived this and quit asking. She didn't want to push him. She could be quiet as well as he could. So they both sat together quietly. They were not exactly in the same frame of mind, and both knew clearly that Berena's lovely, childlike face stood between them.

As soon as the boys came into sight again, Lorenz sprang up and extended his hand to Josepha saying, "God protect you," in such a tone of voice that no wish was perceived in the words.

The maiden opened her purse and laid the money for the fish into his hand and said, "Live well, and come again soon."

"We will come," the little boys called back to her and dipped their wool hats. Then they clambered after their big brother up the mountain.

Josepha remained standing on the dam and watched them go. She could easily see them on the narrow mountain path winding steeply upward, then through the shady fir forest. There they stopped a few moments to catch their breath, and waving down their greeting, they strode over the rushing, foaming creek.

Josepha knew the narrow bridge without rails over which they went and her heart pounded harder till she saw them safely on the other side, climbing, and finally disappearing in the forest.

She wondered whether they would stop at the monastery and thank the holy virgin for protection.

The little church was called *Mary of the Snow.* The little chapel had stood there for over a hundred years. Josepha knew its story. She knew that in the year 1689, alpine cow herders from Rigi had built the chapel to worship there. The mountain dwellers of the vicinity soon used the chapel to worship, and after a hundred years it had been enlarged.

The pope dedicated it, and imparted to the pilgrims the wonder-working *Mary of the Snow.* In the monastery eight monks were placed.

Now it was the year 1805 and the image in the chapel had done many wonders in the last hundred years. Josepha had often heard it told. Would Mary also help her? Could she make Lorenz Waser love her?

Meanwhile the three wanderers arrived home. The boys plunged themselves into their supper, relating their experiences.

Later as the mother sat resting in front of the house door she let her eyes roam across the green pasture. Ulrich slipped onto the lower bench beside her and laid a small black booklet on her lap. He folded his hands on it and asked, "Mother, may I read to you?"

She looked at the strange book and then at his earnest eyes. "What book is it, Ulrich? Where did you get it? How do you know about it?"

He was quiet for a moment, then pressed the book to his cheeks. He seemed to be considering his answer. Holding up his head, he said reverently, "It is the New Testament, Mother. Michael Engler gave it to me."

His mother looked frightened. "Oh child, what if the priest would see it? You know he forbids us to read the Bible. We dare not have it in the house."

"It is not indeed the whole Bible, Mother," said Ulrich soothingly. "Only a part of it. You see, I won't keep it in the house. I'll make a hole under the great stone-pine in the pasture and keep it there. Wouldn't that be allowable, Mother?"

She knew it wasn't right, but it was the common thing to justify oneself through excuses and pretext, so she thought it would do. She did not want to deny her dearly loved child.

She was also secretly curious to read about what he had related to them while eating, so she allowed him to open the Book on her knees and with his arms propped on her lap he began to read the Gospel of Matthew from the first words of the first chapter on.

The sun had long disappeared behind the mountain when he quit reading. The story was so beautiful and wonderful. Many parts they read two or three times, and the mother asked him what Michael Engler had said about it.

Ulrich tried to remember. They both felt very fortunate, but perhaps for this very reason the mother had the anxious feeling that it might be forbidden joy.

As Ulrich shut the book and both went into the house, she said anxiously, "I believe I must confess this to the priest."

At the evening prayer she repeated two prayers more than usual, and as the inner unrest did not go away she asked the holy virgin to forgive her that she had read in the Bible. She tried to excuse herself that she had only listened as Ulrich had read it.

With these thoughts she went to sleep, but already on awakening early in the morning she again had a burning desire to read further into the wonderful Book.

Chapter Three

"Berena."

"Yes, Father."

The young maiden was sitting by her spinning wheel in the summerhouse. Besides her spinning she had also been helping her younger sister with her schoolwork. Berena jumped up and ran light-footed to the long-bearded man who stood at the door of the cow barn. He had all kinds of tools in his hands and was motioning for her to come.

"Hand me the nails," he commanded. "I have things to nail to the stalls."

She obeyed in a friendly manner. She helped her father gladly wherever she could. She had the slight hope she could somehow, sometime, get a smile out of his dark features.

She wished this so much that it was the greatest desire of her life. Berena loved her father. As long as she could remember she had loved him. She didn't know why. He had never exhibited any friendliness to her nor had she ever seen any shown to others. Not even once to her quiet, tender mother, who had so endlessly shown love to him.

His countenance was always dark, his words always hard and cold, his whole being darkness, almost repulsive, and yet, as a small child, Berena had always felt a special drawing to him. Was it pity? Was it the natural drawing of a child to its father?

She always saw pain and sorrow behind his forehead. He was not happy; that was clear, and not only since the death of her mother; it had always been so.

Berena, who felt she would pass away if she had sorrow for one hour, would have given anything if she could for once erase the frown on his face and bring sunshine into his eyes.

She thought, "He is unhappy. Oh, if only I could make him happy." It was the red thread that wove through her whole life; the desire to make her father happy. This was in her mind, and her earnest endeavor was to look for something that would bring joy to his life.

For this reason she had so attentively listened to Michael Engler's story on the island Schwanau, that she might bring a glad message to her father. *What could it be then that makes him so sad—so completely devoid of any joy?*

She looked at him full of fervent love. Her father was a handsome man, tall and stately, strong and inspiring, like her beloved mountain, the Rossberg. But since her trip with Lorenz Waser on the Lowerzer Sea and his mysterious remarks about the old Rossberg, she wasn't so sure about the old mountain.

Berena studied his face, the sharp countenance, the dark eyebrows, and the restless light in his dark eyes. Around the tightly pressed lips lay an embittered countenance, and in the manner that he pounded the nails into the beams lay bitterness, almost wrath. Could she fully trust him?

She could more easily trust Lorenz Waser, she thought. And with these thoughts came a slight feeling of guilt. She could more easily and firmly trust old Michael Engler than her father.

"Father," said she, while holding up a nail for him. "Is it true that our Rossberg sometimes moves?"

"Why do you ask?" he wondered, while slamming down hard with his hammer.

She answered, "Lorenz Waser of the Schwendi-Alp said so."

He considered her a little, thinking. "And what does this Lorenz say?" he asked.

"He says," informed Berena, "that the Rossberg has slid down many times already, and that it could possibly do it again. Do you believe he is right, Father?"

Wendelin laid his hammer aside. "Many, many years ago, a part of the Rossberg slid down. It was the year 1222, then around a hundred years later it happened again. Since then it has remained fairly quiet. Only small rock slides and landslides have occurred."

"And we have nothing to fear, Father?"

"Not as long as the weather stays like it is now. The only thing our mountain cannot bear is long continual rainy weather. Look child, the steep rock-walls that you see, stand on a precipice mass, and under that is hidden the danger in the form of a wide strip of marly soil. This marl band can stand no great amount of water. The water seeps into it and makes the clay soft and then it begins to slide, pulling the rock-precipice which stands on it down with it."

He became almost zealous in his explaining. The knowledge that the hungry eyes of his daughter were fastened on him, stirred him to give all his knowledge on the subject. It almost gave him a feeling of joy to be able to inform someone with his knowledge. But no, for him, for the unfortunate Franz Wendelin, there was no more joy, how did he dare think so?

"I can finish alone, you can go back to the children," said he to Berena, taking the nails from her hand.

Sadly she left. She would have gladly helped him further for it had made her happy to see a slight shine of joy in his dark features. But the shine had vanished as quickly as it had come.

Why? What was tormenting her father?

Regina, her older sister, called from the house, asking her to look after the baby.

So Berena went in, carefully rolling out the little wagon into the sunshine. The little one laughed and stretched out his round arms toward her, and as she bent down and kissed him, his fists hit her fresh cheeks, and grabbing her brown braids he pulled them down. She laughed and they both rejoiced. They loved each other though they were not brother and sister.

A distant relative of her father had brought the child to them. Its mother had died and now the child was being raised at the Spitzibühl.

Regina had resisted the idea. She thought she

had enough work taking care of her own brothers and sisters besides the cattle and the housework. She felt she couldn't add even as much as another little worm to her care.

But then Berena had stepped forward. A baby from her father's family could in no way be refused. This would grieve the baby's father. She would take care of it all by herself. "Give it to me," she begged. "I will take good care of it."

Thus they gave the baby to her. She took him into her bedroom and cared for him day and night. Nothing was lacking him now, and to her indescribable joy he became stronger and rounder day by day, clinging with great tenderness to his foster mother, Berena.

Also her little sister, Eva, loved the baby and as she saw the little wagon standing out in the sun she ran out of the summerhouse and began to pleasantly joke and play with him.

"Are you done with your schoolwork?" asked Berena. "Show me, Eva, what you have written."

The little sister brought her slate, and the boys, Kasper and Michael, recited the poems they had learned. Everything went like clockwork for they knew their sister Berena wanted good work done. But when they got freedom to play, a glad shout broke loose from the two.

Berena herself was more sober than usual. The worries about her father pressed on her soul. Then she also had to think much on the words of the old fisherman on the Schwanau. *If only this Jesus that he told them about would still be alive.* But He was dead. Through much pain He died on the cross.

Thinking of it brought the tears again. If He still lived, oh, how she would ask Him to comfort her father.

She remembered very well the comforting words that Michael Engler had quoted, "Come unto me, all ye that labor and are heavy laden, and I will give you rest!"

Labored and heavy laden! Yes, that was her father. Berena always had the impression that a heavy, unseen burden was pressing upon him. Jesus, the friendly Master, would certainly have taken it from him. But where was He? If only once she could have seen Him.

Berena remembered that an image of Jesus had hung in the little chapel of *Mary of the Snow* in the monastery on Rigi. Mary was shown, holding the dead body of Jesus on her knees.

Suddenly a great longing to see this image came over her. If she could not have the living Jesus, then at least she longed to see the dead one.

Her brothers went up regularly to the meadow where they had made friends with the cattle herders and then had asked permission to go through their pastures to the monastery.

Berena waited awhile till Regina could easily spare her, then asked permission to go visit the monastery.

"As far as I am concerned, you may go," said Regina, "but don't stay too long. Take Eva along, otherwise she is in my way."

Eva was happy. To go with Berena to the holy *Mary of the Snow* was a glorious prospect. She was quickly ready to go, and as Berena needed to bring something from Goldau for her older sister they both struck out on the path.

It was a beautiful day, almost too warm if it hadn't been for the shade on the path. Thus the descent from their house went well. At the fish pond they rested a little, then they strode through Goldau and began the ascent up the Rigi. Soon they came by the mill.

Josepha was standing in her garden looking after the vegetables. As she noticed the two travelers she beckoned to them. "Come and rest a little," she called. "I have fresh milk and fruit."

Eva sprang over immediately. Children always

like treats, and Josepha looked so inviting. She was friendly to both of them and asked where they were going and what for.

Berena informed her somewhat hesitatingly, for she always felt somewhat shy when around the mill daughter, but as she wasn't used to being secretive, she told Josepha everything. Josepha soon knew where they were headed and why.

"You are foolish indeed!" she cried. "What do you want with the dead Jesus? You have the god mother, Mary. You do not need more. Offer to her a candle. Then she will drive out the dark thoughts from your father. Do you have any money with you? If you will go back just a little ways, you will come to the merchant store. There you can buy yourself a little candle."

Berena thanked her for the good advice and quickly ran back down the narrow path. On the merchant's shelves she saw many beautiful things set out. There were colorful images, statues and candles of every size and color. Berena tried a long time to make up her mind among certain things she had set before herself for consideration. Her wax candle must be very beautiful, but the price had to be within the amount of money she had in her little purse, and this wasn't easy.

Finally she decided on a dark red candle with a band of gold and little stars. She laid the money on the table and ascended again to the mill with her "means for joy." She was full of hope. Would not her father receive joy through this light? "The holy virgin will make it so," she thought.

Eva chatted pleasantly as they went up the path together to the Krabel-wall. "See what Josepha gave me," she said. "Something very beautiful." She pulled out of her purse a small oval white pewter box and laid it into her big sister's hand.

Berena pressed on the latch and the cover sprang open. There on a red blanket rested a beautiful, soft lamb with a flag made out of white alabaster. Berena considered it in amazement. "Where did Josepha get this and why did she give it to you?" she wondered.

"Oh, it was so hot in the garden and behind the sea we saw thick black clouds coming up. I was afraid because a storm is so terribly loud. Then Josepha gave me this. She said it is an amulet (a protecting charm). She said that no misfortune can happen to the one that carries it on his person."

"Then I said, 'You must keep it yourself, but she said, I have another one like it and this one I will give to you because I like you and don't want any misfortune to happen to you.' "

Berena nodded. She couldn't help but secretly wonder why Josepha was so good to them. This was so new for her, because until now it had never been so. She laid the red silk blanket again over the lamb and closed the white lid.

"Take good care of it," she admonished, giving the box back to her. "We want to give it to Father. He often has to go on dangerous trips, you know."

Somewhat downcast the child put the gift into her purse. She had wanted to keep it for herself, but she dared not contradict what her generous big sister asked of her.

Silently they went on further. The sun beat down burning hot and only when they came to the shaded cedar forest did they breathe more easily. Here it was also very humid and Eva began to sigh.

"Be brave," encouraged Berena as she pressed her red wax candle to her breast. "The more we suffer the more likely will the god mother regard our prayers."

"Can she do that?" asked Eva in amazement.

Berena considered this, wondering whether she really could do it. She, the holy god mother? Surely she must be able to do anything. It only depended on whether she wanted to. And when she received this candle, indeed then she would surely want to.

Chapter Four

The chapel, *Mary of the Snow*, was packed full of people.

A heavy storm had descended over the mountain. The thunder rolled and echoed threateningly from the bare rock walls. Lightning flashed like red and yellow bands of fire through the dark masses of clouds and then the rain fell in a mighty torrent.

From all over Mount Rigi, from Scheideck, from Staffel, from Rotstock and even from Kulm (villages), the anxious Alpiners had streamed together to pray to the wonder-working Mary for protection of their cattle, pasture, cattle shelters and their houses. Everywhere, they had left at home only the most necessary watchmen and now they all knelt together in close fellowship to bring to the holy virgin their concerns.

The two sisters from Spitzibühl were the first ones there, having sought protection from the oncoming storm. They were now kneeling very close to the god mother on the steps of the altar, with their red candle burning at Mary's feet.

"Make our father happy," came from Berena's lips. Then she was almost terrified at the tone of her voice and over the words which she had spoken. She had never read those words in any of their prayer books. Was she allowed to say those words? Shyly she looked around to see whether anyone had heard her.

Many people were kneeling all around her; cheese makers, ranchers, cattle herders, shepherds, women and children. In a far corner she thought she saw Matthew and Ulrich from the Schwendi-Alp, and beside them, yes, there was Lorenz Waser.

Berena reminded herself that she was in the chapel and was not supposed to be looking around. What must the Capuchin monk think that was kneeling close beside her? Oh, had he heard her perverted prayer?

Quickly she hung her rosary on her arm and began a *Hail Mary.* She needed to make amends for her mistake. Once the storm abated and the chapel emptied again, then she would try to get to the image of the dead Jesus.

She felt an immense longing to do that, almost more, she realized, to be closer to the Son of God than to the god mother.

"Hail Mary, pray for me!" Berena prayed as little Eva pressed at her side. She saw immediately by her other side, to her great amazement and almost terror, a strong dark man which she knew! In spite of the noise in the chapel, and without looking into his face she realized it was her father.

She felt very small beside his herculean figure as they knelt together. And how different were their prayers! Both prayers were perverted, as Berena had said and Eva later related.

Eva heard both Berena's prayer and her father's prayer. Berena's tearful prayer was, "Make our father happy."

Her father, bowed down, contrite and burdened, murmured over and over, "Erase my debt."

The child heard it and saw the strong figure bowing himself and squirming in torment. She was gripped with deep compassion. The small hand groped in her purse for the amulet, and cautiously, full of love, let it slide into her father's pocket as the thought ran through her mind. *So that no misfortune should happen to him.*

The glaring lightning had let up. The thunder rumbled softly in the distance and the rain still fell in torrents. One after the other, the Alpiners started toward home to see how the holy *Mary of the Snow* had protected her own.

Soon the chapel was quiet and almost empty, only Berena stood before the desired image, full of desire for the form of the Saviour.

"Why do you look so intently on Him?" asked the voice of the Capuchin monk beside her. The one from whom she had formerly out of love received the rosary. Terrified she turned around. Had she done something wrong? She bowed to the pious brother. "I love Him so much," she said softly. "I wish He were not dead."

The monk considered her in amazement. How did a simple child of the common people arrive at such thoughts?

"But He had to die for the sins of the world," he answered.

"Yes, I know," she said. "But it hurts me that He isn't here to comfort sad people."

Amazed, he asked, "Are you sad?"

She shook her head. "Not me, but my father."

"What makes your father sad?"

"I don't know, he has never told me," she said sadly.

"I know what makes him sad," said Eva seriously. "He was here in the chapel, right there he was kneeling, where you stand, Father Plazidus, and he was constantly saying, 'Erase my debt.'

"Oh Eva!" cried poor Berena and clasped both her hands to her face.

"What is debt?" asked the child.

"A debt is a crime," explained the monk with feigned harshness. "If your father has a crime on his conscience he will not be free from it until he does heavy penance."

Berena dropped her hands from her eyes, looking at him imploringly. "Oh, what must he do?" she asked anxiously. "Help me Father Plazidus. Can I do it for him?"

The monk shook his head. "This can never a person do for another," he said earnestly. "A child can never do it for its father, not even once. He must make amends for himself. Praying, fasting, self-mortification, making a pilgrimage . . . ."

The peaceful face of the old fisherman on the island Schwanau at this moment became alive in Berena's mind's eye. She heard the ring in his tone and the earnest joy in his voice as he proclaimed, *He suffered and died in our soul's stead to deliver us from hell.*

Immediately she looked at him with eyes of perception as an entirely new light dawned upon her. "But all this has Jesus already done for him. He has died the criminal's death for him; is my father then not free? Didn't He die in my father's place?" she asked anxiously.

It became very warm under the cap of the Capuchin monk. What exceptional questions this child asked! Questions which he till now had never thought about. "Of course He died for him," said he. "But you see your father has a heavy burden on his conscience. He will not be free from it until he makes amends."

"But can not the holy god mother help?" continued Berena. "Can she not make a person happy again? Can't she do anything she wills to do? I have offered her a red wax candle. Will she not want to help? Won't a candle be enough?"

Soft feelings began to stir, of which he had been taught that they dare not be. The monk shook his head. "The holy *Mary of the Snow* will help your father only if he does heavy penance," he explained sharply. His words and his voice were sharp, much sharper than his heart. He, the Capuchin monk of

Mary of the Snow, the faithful son of his church, must be hard and cold like steel.

Berena sat on the steps of the altar, her hands clasped to her face weeping bitterly. She sat there all by herself for a long time. Brother Plazidus had gone out and was walking up to the monastery. And Eva, beckoned outside by the sunshine, was playing among the colorful flowers.

Berena wept and wept. Everything in the world seemed to be so unspeakably sad. Why was everything so hopeless? Why had Jesus died if it didn't do her father any good? And why did the god mother accept red wax candles if she didn't want to help?

With a heart full of love she thought, "If I were the Virgin Mary I would willingly help him and not once would I accept a candle for it!" A little bit of defiance rose in her heart and mixed into her feelings.

Oh me! Evil, bad maiden! She now sighed terrified. *Now I am discontented with the holy god mother. Will she punish my father for this?*

Looking for help she glanced around the chapel. Her gaze became fixed on the image of the dead Jesus and the tears broke afresh from her eyes. *Oh, if only He lived! Then I would trust Him to help poor Father!*

Just then Eva came bouncing in. Running to her big sister she put her arm around her neck and said earnestly, "Berena, Berena, come outside. Ulrich and Matthew from the Schwendi-Alp are here and they say—they say, 'Jesus is not dead, but He lives!'" Her breath came in short gasps as she blurted out the message. She had so rejoiced over it for her sister's sake that she had to share it immediately.

Berena looked startled, then quickly dried her eyes, and taking her little sister by the hand stepped out into the bright sunshine. On the bench sat the two Waser boys with Ulrich holding in his hands a small black book.

"What do you say?" asked Berena, extending to him her hand. "Jesus lives? How do you know that?"

"Out of this book!" said Ulrich joyfully. "You should have this book also, Berena. Everything is in it, all the beautiful things that Michael Engler has told us about; all about Jesus, you know. Not so much about the holy virgin, but that doesn't matter. This is so beautiful and think of it, Berena, it says in here that Jesus became alive again and lives today."

Sitting beside him on the bench she looked into the book. He had opened it to the last chapter of Matthew and with a soft voice was reading it to her. The words rang like music to Berena's ears.

"He is risen from the dead," "He met them," then the last glorious, "lo, I am with you alway, even unto the end of the world." It was the wonderful story of Easter.

Berena's sad heart now pounded, almost bursting for joy because of this precious message. Oh, how must that have been as He met and greeted the women and gave them a commission. She tried to imagine in herself the feelings of those women. First the bitter sorrow, then the rolled away stone. The empty grave, the white shining angels, and then the most beautiful Jesus Himself, alive and not dead, alive and always remaining alive!

With these thoughts Berena was so overjoyed that she sprang up and clasped her hands for gladness and joy. If He lived she could tell Him all her concerns about her father and He would indeed help, for He had been so loving and helpful to others while on this earth. Michael Engler had said so and the Bible said so also.

"I would like to read it again," she said, sighing deeply. "If only I had a book like that."

For a moment an energetic battle of indecision played on the features of Ulrich's face. Suddenly he pulled out his pocket knife and with a couple of strokes he separated the gospel of Matthew from his New Testament. For a second he considered, then extended it to Berena, saying, "It is yours, Berena. Mother and I have already read it all and are ready to start on Mark. You may keep this."

"You dear boy," responded Berena, and with inner joy pressed the pages to her breast. "Oh Eva, now we can read it ourselves."

. . . .

The moon was giving her silvery shine over the quiet monastery as the whole village lay in deep peace. The Capuchin monks rested in their quiet compartments; only one of those compartments was empty.

The monk, Plazidus, lay on the cold, hard floor of the whipping chamber. The blood flowed from many streaks, and still the whip fell heavily on his back. Peace should come again, the peace which he had lost because he had been disobedient to the commandments of his strict mother, the holy church. How had he dared to allow the book to remain in the hands of those children? The church forbade it.

The Bible is not for the common people. And he had seen when they read, he had heard every word. Walking on soft sandals in the cloister he had listened almost breathlessly to what had been said and read on the bench.

Sin! Sin! He dare not listen, he must hinder them! Yet he had not hindered, not with one word nor with one step.

Of the holy virgin there is not much written in it, but that does not matter. All the beautiful things about Jesus . . . sinful thoughts! Away! Away!

How happy it had made those young people to hear that Jesus lives! *Why then has nobody ever told us? Why did we get to hear so little about Jesus?*

Exhausted, Plazidus let the whip fall.

When Wendelin, Berena's father, comes to ask how to free himself from his debt, I will lay heavy penance on him. This will again make the saints and the church satisfied and will again bring peace of heart to myself.

Poor Plazidus! Have you ever called true peace of heart your own? Aren't you always torturing yourself trying to obtain it?

Chapter Five

In Berena's heart there bloomed a wonderful, peaceful happiness. She had read the small gospel which Ulrich had given her, twenty times and it was still always her most desired reading material.

Whenever Regina did not have anything for her to do she would take the baby with her to a quiet place and pull out the pages which she had read many times over. Or, when the baby slept she climbed further up the Ross mountain through the woods and pastures to the highest place, the Wildespitz. There she would sit in her most loved place, under the great iron cross. Holding the pages in her hands she knew she was with her Jesus, entirely alone.

Sometime before, she had been on the island

Schwanau again. The fish had pleased Regina well, so she had sent her younger sister again to old Michael Engler for some more. Oh, how Berena had rejoiced over the assignment. She had so many things to ask him, things which nobody else could answer except dear old Michael Engler.

He made it very clear to her that when a person has an encounter with Jesus, one hears Him speak and he understands. He also explained how Jesus is always there, concerned about everything, loving all mankind, and that He forgives their sins. The last part was indeed the most beautiful!

Now her heart was more glad and free than it had ever been. Jesus had died for her sins and now—this was so glorious! He lived to protect her from sin. He was always, always with her, guarding and helping her.

She also knew now that He had no regard for the number of prayer pearls or for the rosary, but He loved when His children prayed to Him freely from their heart. For this she was so glad. She always had so many things on her heart, burdens which were not expressed in the printed prayer books—the grief her father had, and the cares of her growing foster child. She was troubled about her many unfriendly feelings toward Josepha, and her concern for Lorenz Waser.

Yes, she had concerns for Lorenz Waser.

As Berena sat quietly under the cross with her hands laid around the foot of the iron and her eyes directed on the colossal Rigi across the Golden-Aa meadow, her thoughts rested on Lorenz Waser.

Between the cedar forest and another forest she could see a little bit of the Schwendi-Alp. As she focused her eyes on that tiny bit of land in the distance, she strained to see the lanky form of a boy on the soft green meadow. Her eyes found nothing, yet in her mind she saw his living form before her eyes just as she had last seen him at the Corpus-Christi festival down in Goldau.

He had appeared handsome and grand in his ornamental celebration clothes. At least that is what the other maidens had said. She saw only the amazement in his earnest eyes as she explained to him why she had left the procession.

Indeed, why did she do it? Berena supported her head in her small brown hand, recalling what had transpired.

Formerly she had always gone along in the march. In white clothes and hanging hair she and Eva had walked behind Regina and Josepha. It had always been so year after year. Why was it then different this time?

Ah, it was different. From the beginning Berena did not have the childish joy in the march as formerly. Everything seemed so vainly colorful and noisy; the golden banner, the artistic canopy, the gorgeous garments of the priests, the clanging and the incense. All this she could find nothing about in her gospel, for she knew it almost by heart from reading it so many times.

It seemed so unthinkable that Jesus, who so much loved simplicity and humility and quietness, should have instituted or commanded such a procession. No, this could not have been in His mind. It must have been thought out by people to be able to display such pomp and glamor.

Then suddenly (she could not imagine where she got the courage), she had stepped out of the row of white dressed maidens, and stood, her whole body trembling, at the edge of the street. She stood between the many spectators who accompanied the Corpus Christi procession.[1]

How they had stared at her and condemned her! Josepha, the beautiful, forward, and rich Josepha had

1 Corpus Christi is a Roman Catholic festival in honor of the Eucharist kept on the Thursday after Trinity.

looked around and hissed through her lips, "Heretic!"

"Heretic!" Then the word flew from mouth to mouth. Oh, how terrible it was to hear the despising, scorning and scolding words, and herself alone to be the target of those words.

Never in her life had Berena felt so left alone, so separated, so cast out, and so abandoned. But was she really alone?

In spite of the trembling fear which weakened her body, Berena knew immediately that she was not alone, that someone stood by her side whom she could firmly trust, even though her eye didn't see Him.

"Jesus is here!" rang jubilantly in her heart. "He and I belong together and we are strong even if the whole world is against us."

And while her faith and courage began to be lifted up by this knowledge, there came also encouragement from the outside; a small child's hand slipped into her right hand, partly seeking and partly giving protection, and to her left side, suddenly, tall and straight, a handsome lad in festive clothes.

"Lorenz Waser!" She was so happy to see him in agreement with her that she looked up at him with shining face. Like herself he must have stepped out of the procession. Like herself he must now be despised by the judgment of the multitude. Did he also learn to know Jesus? Her heart pounded, not because of fear, but joy. She bowed herself to her little sister and kissed her rosy lips.

"Where did you come from, Eva?"

The small one smiled at her. "I stepped out of the row because I wanted to be with you. I always want to be with you, Berena."

"But you will be punished in school, dear."

"Punished? When I do what you do? That can't be bad."

"And you, Berena," spoke up Lorenz. "Will not the priest's wrath also be on you? Never has such a thing been allowed."

She looked at him unperturbed. "I don't know," she answered. "It makes no difference, I couldn't do otherwise."

"Why did you do it?" he asked.

Then she related to him what had transpired within her and how she now needed only Jesus without any accessories. She explained how she couldn't go along with anything that He didn't approve of.

Lorenz had listened very attentively then conceded that he could understand, since Michael Engler had told him the same things. But what he didn't understand, was that he needed Jesus the Saviour as redeemer for his sins. Berena perceived it as they discussed it further and it had hurt deeply.

"I don't commit any sins," he had said. "I don't know from what He should deliver me. Don't be angry, Berena, but you don't sin either, you only imagine it."

Berena hadn't become angry, only sorrowful, very sorrowful. And now, sitting high up on the Wildespitz, as she reflected back on their conversation she couldn't do otherwise but fold her hands over her small gospel and pray with half-audible voice, "Oh Jesus, teach Lorenz Waser to become aware of his sins."

Suddenly she perceived a man stepping close to her side, and looking up in terror she saw her father standing in front of her. He appeared more dismal than ever, striking gloom to her heart.

"For whom are you praying?" he asked, with a hint of bitterness.

"For Lorenz Waser of the Schwendi-Alp, Father," she said, the warm blood rising in her cheeks.

The creases between his dark eyebrows deepened. "Why for him? He is not distressed like your father. My child, you should be praying for your own father."

"Oh Father, I do!" cried Berena passionately. "I do it often and with my whole heart. If only I knew better what I should pray for. What is plaguing you, dear Father?"

He extended both hands as if to avert her question. "Quiet, child, quiet. You don't know what you are asking. To know nothing and to keep quiet is all you need to do."

"But you could be so happy," began Berena timidly. "The Saviour Jesus makes all people happy."

"Quiet, child! You believe it! With me everything is over. Your Jesus has nothing to do with such an one as I."

Berena was at once quiet. She sat there without moving, her back leaning against the cross with the gospel resting on her knees. In wondrous beauty the alpine panorama stretched before her; the blooming fields of Lowerz and Goldau in the valley, and the glistening waters of the Zuger and Lowerz seas. The silver cloud formations hovered like a halo around the mountains and in the valleys, above which the well-known Rigi towered.

How peacefully glad and thankful all this made her. And yet she knew, there were those around her who had no peace. He, whom she loved most on the whole earth, was so discouraged, that he believed nothing good could ever happen to him again.

Berena would have given anything to make her father happy. Silently she folded her hands again and prayed, "Jesus, please make my father happy."

She had discarded the rosary, she didn't have any need for it anymore. Michael Engler had none. He had shown her that Jesus Himself was all she needed. A perplexed frown creased her brow. Would Jesus really have nothing to do with her father?

Her gospel must surely have the answer. She paged softly through the little book, looking here and there. Then her eyes fastened on a passage in the ninth chapter. "I am not come to call the righteous but sinners to repentance." She remembered how Michael Engler had read to her these words which had come from Jesus' mouth. Suddenly she knew that her father, with his debt of sin, belonged to the class of sinners who Jesus calls to come to Him. And Lorenz Waser, who did not see any sin in himself, thought he belonged to the righteous.

"What have you there?" asked her father, who had been sitting quietly for a while beside her.

"It is part of the Bible. Oh Father, hear what Jesus says!" She held up the pages and read with a clear voice, "I am not come to call the righteous but sinners to repentance." He calls us Father, you and me."

Shaking his head sorrowfully he answered, "Not me, Berena, not such a sinner as I." He sprang to his feet, then slowly went down the mountain path.

Berena watched with burning eyes, eyes that burned with love and compassion. As she saw the great form disappear into the fir forest she bowed her head again in fervent prayer.

Chapter Six

The day of the Corpus Christi festival in the year 1806 was not soon forgotten in the valley. Josepha, the daughter of the mill, made sure it was not forgotten. She related elaborately how it was that suddenly *that young thing* from Spitzibühl, Berena Wendelin, without saying a word had left her place in the row of rose-wreathed virgins marching in the procession. By this deed she had shown what had been harboring in her heart for a long time, namely defiance and despising of the holy ordinance of the church.

"She is a heretic and if she is suffered any longer in the golden meadow it will no longer be a golden meadow, but terror and destruction will break out in the neighborhood," announced Josepha to anyone who would listen.

This caused a disturbance to break out in the peaceful valley. How had this poison come into their midst?

The priest who heard of the happening at the Corpus Christi festival shook with terror, for he perceived that the holy mother, the church, had been surely severely offended. But because he didn't live in the area, he came only on feast days or festivals. Since Goldau was generally cared for by the Rigi monastery, he commissioned one of the Capuchin monks to investigate the matter and to earnestly punish the heretic. As it turned out, the person commissioned to do the work was the monk, Plazidus.

Regina couldn't believe her own eyes when she saw the brown Kutte (priest's cap) come up the narrow path that led from the fish pond to Spitzibühl. And when the holy man stood before the door and greeted her she bowed her pale head in terror for she knew the evil report that had hissed from angry tongues and that two factions had formed, for and against her sister.

Eva had been sharply reprimanded by her teacher for defiance and disobedience, but she had quietly endured it. Regina had been concerned about the safety of Berena. And now judgment was approaching in the form of Plazidus, appearing as a revengeful judge, so strict, so hard, so demanding for penance.

"Come in, honorable brother," said Regina, mustering all the courage she had. "Rest yourself a little and I will bring you fresh milk."

He lifted a long and thin restraining hand. Brother Plazidus had fasted and chastised himself repeatedly, for he wanted to quench the voice and feeling inside himself which kept on saying, *The young child in Spitzibühl is right, the holy mother and the church are in error. Oh, the sinfulness of such thoughts, away, away with them!* Were not such thoughts much worse for him, the dedicated one to the holy *Mary of the Snow*, than the simple deeds of the ignorant maiden?

But he had come to punish. He must look on the heresy as something black. He must search and investigate whether maybe deeper roots of the heresy poison were stuck in the mind of the child.

"Where is your sister, Berena?" he asked, his voice forcefully harsh.

Regina trembled as she answered, "She is with her little one, I will have her brought in."

"Eva!" she called to the child who was in the garden picking grapes. "Tell Berena to come."

When she came running to her side, she bent

down and whispered, "Tell her to hide her gospel, then come quickly." With a half-curious and half-questioning sideways glance she looked at the monk then went into the house.

Berena came much too soon for Regina's wishes, with her foster child in her arms and Eva by the hand. As she came closer, she appeared indescribably lovely, her cheeks rosy from enthusiastic playing with the little one, her brown hair ruffled from the small one's hands which lay contentedly around her neck. In her fresh looking face there rested an expression of deep joy.

It would take a lot of courage and a rough hand to destroy this peace and joy that shone from the maiden's face. Plazidus felt this and he knew that he was not the man to call this courage his own. How should he go about to make it clear to this joyful child that she was an arch sinner?

"I have to speak to you, Berena," he began. "With you alone. Let the children go."

When Berena gave the little one to Regina the babe cried, reaching his plump, round arms back towards her. His whole heart was set on his foster mother, but Regina firmly took him away, pulling Eva along with her.

Now Plazidus had a free field and he thought, "Now I can be hard." But when an hour later he wandered the long road home he knew that he had not been hard. Not like he who sent and commissioned him with this holy mission had expected of him. The childlike simplicity of the maiden had disarmed him. She simply had no perception of her sin. She couldn't understand why it would be sinful to neglect to do things which the Bible did not command to do.

"Do you pray earnestly to the saints?" he had asked her.

"No, honorable brother."

"Do you use the rosary?"

"No."

"Do you sprinkle yourself with dedicated water, and make the sign of the cross before the image on the road?"

"No."

"Do you read forbidden books?"

This was the first "yes" that came from her lips, a bright clear "yes" exactly as free and open as her "no" had been three times before.

"Show me the books."

Her face registered sadness and pain as she handed them over. Thinking back, Plazidus again saw the sorrowful expression that had come over her childlike face as she obediently drew the pages out of her corset and hesitatingly laid them in his hands.

The small brown fingers rested a moment on the much read over pages, as she beseechingly asked, "May I keep it?"

It was the gospel of Matthew in the German language. Plazidus knew immediately what he owed to the church. "Never again may you read it," he commanded severely. "And to keep you from being tempted I will take it with me."

She looked on sorrowfully as he put it into his own pocket. "Is there anything evil in it?" she asked innocently.

How could a young maiden ask so foolish a question? He had been at a loss for an answer. What should he say? Nothing sensible came to his mind. Finally he had answered, "There are mysterious things in there which you cannot understand without interpretation."

Had he told her the truth? The church taught this but the foolish child before him had appeared as if she wanted to say, "I have read it all and have found nothing mysterious. I understand very well what the Bible says."

At the waterfalls of the Rock-Face creek the monk sat down in the moss and began reading Berena Wendelin's book. He read and read and finally at the last, he found what she had found—revelations of

Jesus, the Son of God.

. . . .

Berena didn't suffer much from the ill-will and hostility of the people. She seldom went down to the valley and knew that she had good friends at Rigi who took her part in spite of the cry of heretic.

After the monk had taken away her book, she went to the Schwendi-Alp and asked permission to read with Ulrich and his mother out of his book. She was so very hungry for the words of the Bible since Plazidus had taken away her Gospel of Matthew.

Then Ulrich went and cut out both the Gospel of Mark and Luke and laid them into her hands, saying, "Take it Berena, we have read it many times. Isn't it true, mother, that we have enough with having the Gospel of John and all the rest?"

The mother had nodded and embraced Berena as she was leaving. Ulrich Waser had given Berena a precious gift.

She loved Berena almost as her own child, and nothing would have pleased her more than to see Berena and Lorenz become a pair. It seemed so natural to her. Could they do otherwise but to love each other?

"It is time for you to choose for yourself a young lady," said Lorenz's father a bit later to Lorenz after Berena had gone and they were working together. "Mother and I are growing old and the Schwendi-Alp needs young people who have strength."

Lorenz quietly loaded the hay on the wagon, remaining silent.

"Josepha Hurliman is now seventeen years old and is a beautiful maiden. She is rich besides and also good. See to it that nobody snatches her away from you."

"Good?" asked Lorenz. "Do you know that, father? Berena from Spitzibühl is good, and she, father, is the one I love."

Old Father Waser stuck his hay-fork forcefully into the ground, looking searchingly at his son. "The heretic?" cried he threateningly. "Don't you think of bringing her over our threshold. We don't need any misfortune on the Schwendi-Alp."

"Misfortune, Father? Fortune will come with her. Don't you know that God is with her and, she with God?"

Lorenz surprised himself. Never had the difference between Josepha and Berena been so clearly impressed in his mind as now when he questioned his father's judgment.

This had been the cause of the turmoil of indecision in his mind. Josepha attracted him, then repulsed him. Berena was always attractive to him.

One thing stood between him and Berena—her faith. He couldn't share this faith with her. When she spoke of Jesus, the Saviour of sinners, he couldn't understand her. Or was it that he didn't want to?

Yes, he didn't want to. Lorenz Waser didn't want to call himself a sinner. He was righteous, good and honorable. Everybody considered him so, why didn't Berena also? And how did God's judgment relate to this question?

That Lorenz took God's judgment at all into consideration was caused by Berena. It was also her fault that he constantly caught himself wondering how he would give account of his doings and of his words. It made him uncomfortable, for always the question came, is this right in God's eyes? Is this like Jesus would do?

He tried to ward off these questions but they always came back, pressing on him and against his will he felt forced to answer them.

When his old father pressed on him the desirableness of Josepha, he flared up sharply against him. Then he thought of Jesus and how He was subject to His own parents, for Jesus had said, "Learn of me for I am meek."

Berena had often told him this and he had heard his own mother and Ulrich read it.

He knew that he should not curse when everything seemed to go wrong at work, and that at confession he should tell the priest the whole truth. He knew also that he should not hate his father, and yet when his father spoke so despising of Berena, saying, "I will chase you from house and home if you undertake to bring in that heretic," then his feelings many times couldn't be differentiated from hate.

Recently when his father said, "The spoiled harvest with the abundance of rain come only because of the heretic, Berena Wendelin," he had almost raised his hand against him.

It had rained much, it seemed without end. The water poured from the sky. The first harvest of hay was brought in dry, but since then it had rained unceasingly all summer long.

. . . .

Ulrich, the little thinker, thought often of the words of the old fisherman on the Schwanau, when he said, "The old Rufiberg cannot endure a lot of rain." Many times he had cast a worried look toward the mountain to see whether it had already moved. No, so far it seemed to be firm, secure and unmovable in its proud magnitude.

It wouldn't have made much difference to Ulrich what happened to the old Rufiberg if it wasn't that the white walls and red roofs of Spitzibühl were so close to it.

And on the Spitzibühl was Berena whom he loved with all the fervor of his lively little-boy heart. Berena, who conversed with him about Jesus and the Bible. Berena, who so courageously had stepped out of the procession.

"That was absolutely not right of her," said Matthew. "You know that for this, Plazidus has laid penance on her."

"Indeed, but believe me, he didn't do it willingly, he had to," said Ulrich in defense.

"Josepha is better than Berena," continued Matthew. "Josepha gives us cake and fruit."

"I can do without her cake and fruit," retorted Ulrich. "She has an evil look about her."

"Oh you, only heretics have that. Berena Wendelin is a heretic."

"Quiet, would you keep quiet, you bad boy!" Anger boiled in the old Waser's heart. The two boys were often in strife concerning this. There were differences of opinion on this, on the Schwendi-Alp as well as in the valley.

"Pure discord," said the old Waser. "And all

because of this new heretical teaching." He punished both boys hard, but Ulrich the hardest.

He excused himself to his wife by saying, "He is the elder." But Ulrich knew it would have been so even if he had been the younger. He was not on his father's side of the division. This made him bitter against his father and brother and when he met Berena he told her his troubles. This made her very sad.

"The Bible says we should love each other, Ulrich," said Berena. "Try to be kind and good to your father and brother Matthew."

He promised to do it. He could never turn down the friendly requests of Berena and for a while he succeeded in being forbearing toward his brother.

There was much unrest now in all this area that seemed to the people almost like paradise. Outwardly it appeared only like a paradise. In the people's hearts there was much stirred up hate and hostility.

At the Aabach mill, evil thoughts were spun out. Josepha Hurliman contemplated and studied day and night on how she could end the good fortune at the Spitzibühl.

When someone studies on how to do evil, then he quickly has a helper. The enemy who is always prepared to sow tares, and the plans that are produced are devilish.

Chapter Seven

At the Spitzibühl there was company, choice company thought the children. Josepha, from the Aabach mill was welcomed for she always brought something for each one.

Josepha was shown to the best easy chair in the parlor. "A person can't work in the garden since it has rained so much this whole week, but in this room it is very pleasant," she said, smiling sweetly.

She commented how the coffee tasted so good, praising Regina for the wonderful tasting cake, all the while chatting brightly of this and that. "I must also see the house and barn. I know that everything is super clean and that is how I like to see it."

With much pride, Regina showed her their

possessions and home with her father following along, explaining what she desired to know. It seemed almost to brighten him a little.

But Berena's eyes, sharpened by love, noticed an anxious shyness in him which seemed as if he was guarding himself carefully, so as not to be influenced by Josepha's cheerfulness. "Why?" she wondered.

After their tour of the farm, they gathered together in the living room. Berena had her foster child on her lap, Regina was busily at her knitting and the little children sat on their low benches.

Josepha chatted pleasantly. "So that no misfortune should happen to me on the way home I have with me a safety charm." She pulled something out of her vest and laid it down toward Wendelin, watching him closely.

"Why Father, that's exactly like yours!" cried Eva, who was leaning on her father's knees. She reached into his jacket and pulled out the oval white tin box that Josepha had given her earlier and laid it on the table. "Exactly the same! Oh, look Father, inside they are also almost the same!"

She opened both boxes and wonderingly compared the red silk covering of the one and the blue silk covering of the other. The white alabaster lamb and the flag were the same in both.

The child had no premonition of the stage she was setting.

Deep silence filled the room for a short moment. Snow white to the lips, sat Wendelin.

Josepha rose from her chair immediately, towering over him like an angel of vengeance, her face flaming red and her beautiful countenance completely changed into an appearance of barely hidden satanic glee.

"Murderer of my father!" she cried, pointing with her finger to both amulets. "Deny it if you can!"

An agitated cry resounded through the little room. It came from Berena's lips.

Rising quickly she laid the child into Regina's lap and fled to her father's side, flinging both arms around his neck and covering his pale forehead with loving kisses from trembling lips.

"Father, Father, tell her to go! Go out, Josepha! How can you, oh, how can you speak such horrible words?! Regina, tell her to go!"

Mortal terror was seen and heard in her words, voice and eyes; anguish for her beloved father. It could cause their father's death to hear such a terrible accusation.

Regina rose to her feet. She tried to be very calm and sensible. "What grounds do you have for such a serious accusation?" she asked in a stern voice.

"How can you think such a dreadful thing?"

Once again Josepha pointed a white finger to the two open boxes. "The box with the red covering belonged to my father; the one with the blue was found close to the body. The person with the red covering must be the murderer," she said slowly in a hard, cold voice.

Eva began to weep but the meek Berena, trembled with fear.

"Deny it if you can!" cried hard-hearted Josepha again, stepping closer to Wendelin.

He didn't stir or move an inch, sitting there bowed; pale, moaning, the appearance of a criminal.

"Father! Father!" cried Berena pressing her brown head against his deeply bowed head. "Say that she is lying! You didn't do it! You are not a . . . ." The horrible word refused to come over her lips.

But with zealous satisfaction Josepha finished the clause, "a murderer," she said cuttingly.

"Josepha!" As a cry of death, it came from Berena's mouth. She let go of her father and grasping Josepha's arm, she looked pleadingly at her.

Then suddenly her father's voice came to her ears, without any feeling or expression; she would never forget the fearful tone. "Berena, your father *is* a murderer."

Slowly, slowly, Berena's senses came back to

her. A deep fainting spell had compassionately taken her into its arms when she heard those dreadful words. Now her thoughts were coming back. *Oh fearful thoughts, go away! Oh, that I might never need to think again, never wake up to life which is so void of comfort, so despairing.*

"Your father is a murderer."

Whose father? Surely not mine . . . mine . . . Berena Wendelin's beloved father? Can a person love a murderer? Impossible!

"Your father is a murderer."

This dreadful lie! Who had spoken this dreadful lie? Who could dare take such words into his mouth?

Berena tried to dismiss the thought that she had heard those terrible words; it must have been a stranger's voice, she couldn't comprehend it.

Was she among strangers? Wasn't she at home? Shyly she opened her eyes, and then . . . everything became clear with perfect sharpness.

Beside her bed, his face white to his lips, looking anxiously at her, sat her father.

"Your father is a murderer."

With a slight cry, Berena turned away from her father and turned her face toward the wall.

. . . .

Berena was not sick, the young energetic daughter from the Spitzibühl. Before long the body was fresh and healthy like before, but the soul . . . how was it with her soul?

It is impossible to love a murderer. This conviction was firmly embedded in Berena's mind and pressed like a heavy burden on her soul. Wherever she went it rang in her ears, "Your father is a murderer."

She estranged herself completely from her father. Did they have anything in common anymore? Were they not separated for time and eternity?

Berena had never imagined anything to be more terrible and sinful than murder. She had for years been living under the same roof with a murderer, and never knew it.

When she saw her father, she seemed to see blood on his hands. Shyly she avoided any communication with him, and under no circumstances did she allow him to take her little one into his arms as formerly.

Now she understood why her father was wretched and that he considered it impossible to become otherwise.

"Such a sinner as I, Jesus would not accept." She could still hear his despairing voice say these words when they were there under the cross on the Wildespitz. And now she could only bow her head and in her deepest inner heart agree. *Such a sinner? No.*

She would so gladly have gone to Michael Engler with her inner torments, but the rainfall which fell almost daily, hindered her from going.

She also feared meeting Josepha, for the thought of her put her in a condition of hot anger. *Anger, hate, bitterness . . . oh how many evil things does a young maiden's heart have room for?*

. . . .

Josepha's heart burned like wild fire. As she went through the house and yard looking after her things she constantly had a feeling of hateful triumph. Had she not triumphed gloriously? Was not the road now open for her own good fortune?

Josepha had gone through much heartache the last while. She saw how Lorenz's heart was inclined toward Berena, and bitter feelings of hate, jealousy and ill-will festered in her heart. These feelings increased week after week, giving her no rest. Finally they drove her to evil planning. That simple Berena, from Spitzibühl, dare not capture the prize which she, the beautiful rich owner of the mill, desired.

The conditions seemed to be ripening to her

advantage. Berena's heresy was much to her liking, though she saw that Lorenz himself was a little influenced by her. He also gladly read the Bible, and at times neglected the holy ordinances of the church. At the Corpus Christi festival he had incurred the wrath of the church the same as she.

But Lorenz was subject to his father, and he was against all heresy. He would not allow it in his home and under no circumstances would he receive a heretic for a daughter-in-law.

Josepha tried to make sure that these thoughts and conclusions became established and nourished in Lorenz's heart. She spoke to him about it often, informing him of Berena's offense and crime, and of the terrible curse that lies on all heresy.

Putting herself in the light of being most desirable and worthy of love, she was as attentive and obedient as any father could wish his daughter to be.

She knew with certainty that she had won the elder, that he would receive none other but her, but what about Lorenz?

That was the critical point. She couldn't get away from thinking that Lorenz's love for Berena was in a constant state of growth, and that his father's threats to chase him from house and home didn't dampen him. She must plan something else, something that would forever separate Schwendi-Alp from Spitzibühl.

Thus evolved the devilish plan with the two boxes. Her father was the owner of the one with the red covering. She remembered very well that horrible day. Early on the day of the church festival, before her father had gone, he had shown her the wonderful beautiful lamb and said, "I am blessed, I carry an amulet with me and nothing bad can happen to me."

And then the horrible moment when early the next morning the body was fished out of the red Rock-Face creek. She had carefully sought for the amulet… it was not to be found.

Later someone found it, along with the other with the blue silk covering, which till then they had never seen. Both lay above on the incline close to the bridge which had no railing, over the steep, downward flowing red Rock-Face creek.

To whom did the second amulet belong? Everything depended on the answer to this question, for the owner of the second amulet must surely be the murderer.

The investigators seized both amulets and set in action a most thorough investigation. No leads were found. The murderer remained concealed. Yet it was clear that it was a murder, and not suicide, for tracks around the bridge showed two people in strife.

Who was the murderer? After these many years the question remained still unanswered.

Gradually grass grew over the place of the happening and people quit questioning and searching. Both amulets were given to the daughter of the murdered one to keep.

Josepha made use of them in her wicked plan. She was not trying to discover or uncover the murderer, but only to expose a certain man, Berena's father. If he could be shown to be the criminal, then she was sure Spitzibühl and Schwendi-Alp would be forever divided.

She knew Berena, and on this she built her plan. She schemed, knowing that her small amulet would soon find its way into the father's pocket for all Berena's love culminated in him. And then the thing would be settled.

No swearing to his innocence would deliver him when the amulet would be found in his possession, for when it would be said that the daughter of the mill owner had presented the amulet to Eva, she would deny it. And who would the people believe, the child or herself?

Everything had progressed with such success that Josepha herself had been surprised. She had never imagined Franz Wendelin to really be the murderer.

She was dumbfounded with astonishment at his frank confession. Was not the holy god mother standing on her side helping her?

Josepha herself was very elated. Nothing stood in her way anymore. She also wanted to be generous now, knowing it was unnecessary to bring charges against Wendelin, for she knew Berena well enough that she would certainly now be ashamed to defile the honorable name Waser with blood by marrying Lorenz.

One thing she still wanted to do for her security, actually two things. She would buy a letter of indulgence for the harm that she had brought over Spitzibühl, and offer a wax heart to the *Mary of the Snow* so that she would incline the heart of Lorenz Waser toward herself.

Chapter Eight

Storms and rain had raged for days.

"This is something we often think of these days," said the goat-herding boys, who with the cow-herders, let their herds graze on the wet, green meadows of the Rufiberg. "In bygone days, the old Rufiberg sprang cracks and fissures when we had such quaking as we're seeing now. It would seem almost as if it could happen again."

Then the rains stopped.

It was a sunny day on the afternoon of September 2, 1806. People and cattle utilized it enthusiastically and rejoiced for the long withheld sunshine. The herders started yodeling and the birds chirped happily in the branches.

"The people should not have been so fearful as to move away from the mountain," said Alois, the cow-herder to the old Gisler. "It was cowardly of them."

The older one shook his head. "I don't know," he said doubtfully. "It was caution, for sure, but not cowardice. Lately it has cracked very much in the mountain, Alois."

"Yes certainly, I heard it. But now the sun shines again and everything is secure."

"Everything secure?" questioned the old one. "May the holy virgin protect us. The cattle are restless today, Alois. See how Rosa holds her head, sweeping with her tail . . . "

Alois sprang after the animals. Today they all pressed downward, but the better grass was higher up the mountain. Rosa must be guided upward then the others would follow her.

"Who is coming?" called Alois, while still running. "Look Father Gisler, there is a man coming up."

The old man looked around with his sharp eyes. "It is Wendelin," he answered. "How he drags himself and how bowed-over he walks, as a very old man and yet he still has strong, young blood."

"The path is worn smooth and slippery," noted Alois. "It makes hard going for one like him. Franz

Wendelin is a heavy man."

By now the wanderer had reached the meadows.

He looked as if he were about to die; pale and thin of face, the mighty form bowed over. The path appeared toilsome to the weary man. In passing he greeted them.

The old shepherd stretched out his hand to him. "Sit down a little, Wendelin. Where are you going?"

"To the Wildespitz, to the cross up there."

"Take a little time, Wendelin, you will not get there like this. You are tired to the bones."

Wendelin nodded. "Yes, tired," he said. "Tired to death." There was a hopeless tone in his voice.

"Then rest here."

He shook his head. "I have no time to rest. I must go up . . . up." As he went on he lifted his hat and in doing so a bunch of lavender flowers that Berena had stuck in the hat-band, fell to the ground.

He saw it and sorrowfully turned back. "Never more will she put flowers in my hat-band. My child despises me. All people despise me. God despises me."

Groaning deeply, he climbed further. How much he had atoned for, mortified himself for, prayed and made pilgrimages, offered . . . yet the debt remained. Would God's wrath against him never be laid to rest? Would he have to suffer torture forever, here and on the other side?

"I have deserved it, oh I have deserved it," he groaned. And then he listened to the extraordinary chirping of the birds about him. They fluttered and hurried around so strangely restless and the sound of the herds coming up from below had a shrill unmelodious ring. Or was all this because there was no inner harmony in himself?

A peculiar cracking sound burst through the mountains. Wendelin stopped climbing momentarily, making the sign of the cross.

"This is an eerie day! God be with me! God? Would God be concerned about someone like me? Woe is me."

He climbed the last rock steps to the cross and sank down exhausted at the foot of the cross.

Me, a poor mortal, who can make me free from my debt?

That day years earlier, which had been more eerie than this one to Wendelin, came back again, alive in his memory.

How the storm had raged in the cedar forest. How it shook those old trees, lightning flashed through black clouds and the thunder sounded through the mountains. How the red Rock-Face creek roared.

Raging and foaming it plunged to the valley.

The bridge that led across it was narrow and without railing. Could a person dare to go over it in the changing light of the lightning? The blinding light of lightning flashed again. It revealed in sharp clearness two men at the edge of the waterfalls and two shiny objects in their hands, two shiny boxes of white tin.

"Let's venture it," said the one. "Our amulets will protect us."

"Do you believe that?" laughed the other. "I have nothing for such nonsense, God protects me."

"Take heed, Franz!" called the first one. "Your wife teaches you such heretical thoughts. I have known for a long time that she is a heretic!"

Oh yes, it was true. Franz Wendelin had likewise known this for a long time. But now that he heard it from someone else he was overcome with anxiety, that the thing might become public and his most beloved wife would have to suffer persecution and bitter heart-ache from the church and the world. He would have to avoid that at any cost.

"She is not a heretic!" he had shouted.

"She definitely is!" shouted Hurliman. "I know it and I will tell the priest!"

"That you will not!" said Wendelin raising his

arm threateningly.

Then the miller plunged on him. The drunkenness which had come over him from drinking too much at the church festival was not yet gone and therefore his blood boiled quickly and he began to furiously wrestle with Wendelin.

Wendelin withstood him with all his might, and because he was sober and of herculean build he had the advantage, and then . . . then came the disaster.

In his striving, Hurliman stepped over the edge of the bridge and plunged down into the raging deep. In the glaring shine of a lightning stroke, Wendelin once saw the dark form being tossed here and there in the white foam, and a fearful cry rang through the dark forest. Then everything was quiet.

Even the storm had quieted down. Franz Wendelin strode over the bridge, and like in a dream wandered toward home. He didn't think about his amulet. In their struggle both had fallen to the ground.

Oh the bitter days, weeks, and years that followed then! With dread Wendelin brought them back to remembrance.

His quiet wife had died and they had carried her down to the cemetery by the sea. He still had the children, and he could have had joy in them. But the nagging hurt in his heart and the tormenting cry of his conscience . . . *murder, murder.*

Not for an instant was he free from the feeling of guilt. The brightest moments of his life were when Berena showed him her love, and whenever she was near him she always did, but then she had not known that he was a murderer. And when she found out—he quaked and shook with a deep cutting hurt in his heart—since then it was over with her love. His child avoided him and despised him, and if she did, how much more did God?

Oh God, have mercy on me! The one petition in the Lord's prayer; how does it go? "Forgive us our debts."

Can God then forgive debts? The priest says, "After much mortification, praying, fasting"—indeed but all this he had tried and still there was no forgiveness. The debt weighted him down heavier than ever.

What shall I do? Tell me, God. I long for deliverance! Forgive me my debt. I want to do everything, everything that thou desirest!

The tormented man knelt at the cross, clutching it with both hands. His whole body shook in longing desire. The dark eyes gazed beseechingly toward heaven. "Help me, God! Oh, cleanse me from my debt!"

Immediately there stood before his soul a shining clear word, a word out of the holy book that his quiet wife had liked to read, a word that he had often heard from her because it was one of her favorites, **"The blood of Jesus Christ his Son cleanseth us from all sin."**

The words fell like balsam on his wounded heart. He spoke the words out loud again and then again, each time louder and firmer, as though he wanted to teach them to the mountains and clouds around him.

Clean from all sin, also from murder and secrecy, it makes me pure, but how?

Also on this question he immediately had the answer. **"Through faith. You only need to believe it, you have nothing to do. We become righteous without the works, only through faith."**

He believed even now to hear the voice he had heard. Then, thanksgiving and exultation streamed suddenly into his heart. Pure through the blood of Jesus . . . he could believe it . . . he did believe it!

. . . .

Meanwhile, also at the Spitzibühl, a child lay on the ground. Berena had seen her father go, so bowed down, so full of hopeless pain, she could hardly bear the sight.

The fervent child-love wanted to rise up inside her. She yearned to plunge after him, to throw her arms around his neck and kiss his poor sorrowful face.

But he was a murderer! Can a person kiss a murderer? Is it lawful to love him? Suddenly Berena knew that she loved this murderer. Even though she had steadfastly told herself the opposite and acted accordingly. She knew now that deep in her heart the old love burned unquenched, almost deeper and more fervently than before, because it was mixed with compassion.

But dare that be? Was he not a sinner? Berena was convinced that if in the confessing seat she would whisper it to the priest, he would dictate severe punishment. But what would Michael Engler say? Often his views were different than the priest's. And what would Jesus say about this? Oh, if only she knew, that would settle the matter.

Berena laid the child in the cradle and gave him his bottle of milk, then pulled her Gospel out of her corset. Earnestly she began to seek, now in Mark, now in Luke. There must have been a case when Jesus said something about a murderer. She became warm in her earnest seeking and yet did not find what she was looking for.

"Berena," suddenly said a well-known voice close by her side. She looked up, frightened.

"Lorenz, oh Lorenz!" she cried in confusion.

He sat beside her on the grass. "Why are you so frightened?" he asked. Then he answered it himself. "Because you are so in earnest. What are you looking for, Berena?"

Then she poured out to him her whole heart. She was so glad to finally be able to do it and Lorenz was a good listener. His blue eyes rested with compassion on her agitated features.

When she had finished he said much more earnestly than was normal for him. "Many think so like you have thought, poor child. My father thinks so, but let us leave that. Berena, I have never thought so, never."

She looked on him with gratitude, then a shadow came over her face. "Then does everybody know about it?" she asked.

"The people whisper much. Josepha may not have remained quiet, or the children; you know they were all present."

Berena sighed. "Then all the people in the valley and in the mountains look despising on my father, on my poor, dear father." She put her hands to her face and broke into tears. He tenderly looked into her face.

"Don't cry!" he said.

She took her hands from her eyes and looked toward him expectantly. "Lorenz, do you know what Jesus said concerning murderers?" she asked. "I mean, whether a person dare love them?"

Lorenz was sorely disappointed in himself. Gladly would he have told her what she wanted to know but he knew so little of the words of Jesus. And to answer her, he didn't trust himself to tell her where to find it in the Scriptures. Having no counsel to give, he didn't answer. From Berena's brown, childlike eyes, a disappointed expression shown through.

"Did He never have any contact with a murderer?" she questioned, searching her own memory. "He had forgiven the sins of so many people, was there never a murderer among them?"

Lorenz searched his memory. "Wasn't there a murderer crucified with him?" he suddenly asked, considering what he remembered hearing Ulrich read to their mother.

Berena brightened. "Yes, even two, but . . . " and already the disappointment showed in her face. "He had not spoken any words with them."

"Yet . . . yet, Berena," said Lorenz earnestly. "He had, I know it for sure. To the one of them He had spoken something wonderfully beautiful. My mother rejoiced over it very much. I remember she said to Ulrich, 'In the Gospel that you gave to Berena, which we had read earlier, it doesn't say it.' And Ulrich had said, 'No, Matthew doesn't relate it, but Luke does.' How sad Berena, that you don't have Luke, then we could read it together."

"But I do have it!" cried Berena joyfully. "Here it is. Ulrich gave it to me. Oh Lorenz, look for the place, find it quickly! It must be far toward the end, for I have already read it to the middle and have not found anything of it."

Earnestly he took the small booklet, paging to the last chapters. "Here! Berena, here it is! Come, let's read the story."

The two heads bent over the book so that the blond and the brown hair almost touched each other. Both of them read the wonderful, glorious story out loud; how Jesus on the cross forgave the murderer and promised he would be in paradise with Him that day.

" 'Today thou shalt be with me in paradise.' How wonderfully beautiful! Jesus must have an indescribable fervent love for the poor criminal that he took him as the first one with Him into paradise.

'With me!' He wanted to have him close by Himself, very close!"

"Why did He accept the one and not the other?" wondered Lorenz.

"Oh Lorenz, that is very clear," said Berena, looking into the book. "See, the one blasphemed the Saviour, but the other prayed for His help."

Once more they read the whole passage together. Then suddenly, as if enlightened, Berena exclaimed, "This must Father also do! Then he will be free from his debt burden. Oh, Lorenz, Lorenz, run after him. See, I can't leave the child. You run! He has gone to the Wildespitz. Go after him and tell him the glad message. Jesus loves him, and will forgive him his debt if he asks him to!"

Her face glowed in her excitement. Lorenz Waser looked on her with amazement. It was impossible for him to deny her.

"I'll go," he said leaping up from the ground. "Listen, didn't something crack in the mountain? It is very humid. Look, there come your goats, running! Something seems eerie to them in the meadow, as though something is brewing, Berena."

She looked at him, begging beseechingly, "Go to my father, Lorenz, please, please."

As he went and disappeared into the fir forest,

she sank to her knees and prayed, "Oh Lord, forgive me that I have been so hard on my father. Saviour, bring him down again to me and help me that I may show to him how very much I love him!"

Chapter Nine

Plazidus had gone to the Schwanau and had read the mass in the chapel. After having a long conversation with Michael Engler, he was now on his way home, deep in thought. The peace this old man appeared to have would surely be wonderful. And he seemed to have it effortlessly, living his quiet life earnestly and happily.

Plazidus, the always striving, fighting, and self-tormenting monk, had asked him, “Are you really never afraid, old Engler? Not from eternal damnation, and never once of purgatory?”

Then the clear blue eyes so full and free, looked on him with a blessed smile as he had answered, “I know that if my Saviour would call me today, that I would go to be with Him in paradise."

The solitary wanderer in the brown cowl (monks' cap) stopped his ascent. He climbed upon the wall where he had a clear view of the Schwanau.

How wonderfully beautiful the island lay, played about by the waves of the sea, and overlooked by the mighty Mythen mountains which towered heavenward.

So quiet and peaceful, the island matched its inhabitant. Oh, who wouldn't like to have such peace, who so peacefully and serenely could look death into the eyes. *What is the difference between me and that foolish old man?*

"I have Jesus, and you have the church," the old man had said during their conversation.

The young monk now considered the old man's words, "I have Jesus, you have the church." Does that make the difference? How simple and glorious it must be to reverence only One. Only One, instead of countless saints of men and women which the church sets as patterns; saints of which the Bible says nothing.

Plazidus, now familiar with the Bible, would so gladly have used it as his only plumb line! But that wouldn't do, for the church teaches otherwise, and what the holy church teaches is infallible.

Michael Engler kept himself only to the Bible.

Would he dare do the same?

Plazidus leaned his back against the stone wall, breathing deeply. An emotional weight pressed heavily on his heart; he was visibly uneasy in spirit.

Suddenly he noticed it was getting dark. The air was humid and heavy, stifling heavy. He pulled out his watch. A quarter till five.

Listen, what was that?

An unusual whirring and flapping of wings sounded in the air as a host of birds were fleeing from the direction of the Rossberg toward Rigi. In fright they fluttered over his head, hiding themselves in the trees of the cedar and birch forests.

What was that?!

A horrifying crack resounded through the mountain air. Then a loud roar such as Plazidus had never heard in all his life, nor imagined.

With both hands he clung to the bare rocks of the Krabel-wall and peered over toward the old Rufiberg. He was overtaken with horror.

The forests became alive with vibrant movement as a colossal thunder clap echoed through the air, reverberating in a thousand mountain chasms.

With a great roar and wild clatter, the peak, along with the rock mass under it, moved with lightning swiftness and plunged down toward

Goldau.

"Oh God, have mercy!"

Rocks, the size of a house, and great rows of trees, arched through the air with the speed of an arrow. Houses, people, and cattle were flung through the air.

Almost stunned, Plazidus sank to his knees. The air was pressingly heavy so that he was barely able to breathe. The plunging mass of earth took its course till far up on the Rigi a dreadful reddish-brown cloud of dust descended over the valley, enveloping the avalanche in dreary darkness.

The usually quiet waters of the Lowerzer Sea, rose up like a wall as a mass of dirt and rocks from the mountain suddenly filled a part of the sea. The huge waves swept over both small islands, rolling over to the other shore and tearing along with it everything in their way.

Is the day come in which the desperate will cry, "Ye mountains fall over us and hills cover us?"

"Today, today, thou shalt be with Me in paradise."

Then it was quiet. Deep, deep quietness.

In a few dreadful moments the fearful devastating work was done. The golden meadow and its lovely surroundings disappeared and nothing met the eye except ruin and rubble.

Goldau, Bursinger, Rothen and Lowerz were all buried under dirt and rocks, a massive grave for hundreds of people.

. . . .

Solitary and unharmed, the iron cross on the Wildespitz towered upwards. Clinging to the foot of the cross was a man of herculean stature, but struck almost to death by the paralyzing horror of the moving mountain.

Beside him knelt his daughter. "Father, are you alive? Oh, dear father, wake up, be alive! Berena is here and wants to show you her love for you."

Her anxious, imploring words finally brought him to his senses. With confused dark eyes he looked at her, his mind hardly functioning. Suddenly his thoughts found a firm support.

"The blood of Jesus Christ his Son cleanseth us from all sin."

He spoke the words clearly and plainly two times, and the second time with strength and great joy! His white face had the same peaceful look as that of the old Engler on the Schwanau. He smiled on his daughter. "Berena, my child, do you also forgive your poor father?"

Sobbing the maiden hid her face on her father's breast. It was impossible for her to say a word.

Suddenly he regained some strength to speak.

With a weak, understandable voice he related plainly the happenings of that fearful night on the bridge of the red-rock creek. He kept nothing back. He wanted Berena to hear it and also the old Waser and Plazidus who had accompanied Berena to the cross. They all listened with increasing emotion.

"Tomorrow I had intended to give myself over to judgment. But now it won't be. Death comes in other ways than through hanging."

"Father, Father," sobbed Berena. "Can, oh can you forgive me, that I could think so evil of you? Oh say that you forgive me."

The large, dead-tired hand sought to stroke her, to press her brown head to his breast. "My beloved child, my life's only joy," whispered the dying lips.

She felt that he left her and she knew that she dare not, nor could she, keep him. Her clearest feeling in this moment was thankfulness. "Dear, dear father, today, yet today, you will be with Him in paradise."

Yet once more the tired eyes looked at her happily. "With Jesus yet today . . . ."

Berena listened intently for more words; none came. Plazidus tenderly laid his hand on his head and softly said, "He is in paradise."

Chapter Ten

Later, Berena did not know how she could have survived that day, that dreadful September second, and its fearful happenings. Oh, the hours full of torment she had endured. First the horrible moment when a strong air movement came from above which was the forerunner of the plunging mountain.

From before her eyes it had snatched away the cradle with her dear little one, taking it flying through the air. She cried out loud, but then knew nothing more till a strong hand quickly pulled her into the house. Later she found out it was Regina's hand. There had been suddenly over her, beside her, and under her, a terrible sound, a thundering roar.

When the fearful minutes were finally over,

and they had come to their senses, she found herself with Regina and their small sister securely locked into their bedroom. The air pressure had forced in the window panes and a cloud of dust had partially settled in the house. But Regina, Berena, Eva, and the two little boys, Kasper and Michael, were unharmed; and the house still stood, firm and secure.

Regina read a prayer of thanksgiving out of the prayer book, but Eva cried and called for Father and the baby.

Berena sprang up on her wavering feet and cried, "I will go back for them, I will look for both of them."

Regina had not been able to keep her from going. She could not leave the house and children herself, so she finally let her go.

Berena began searching. She had to find the child. He couldn't be very far, but, but . . . Berena couldn't finish the thought. How, or in what condition would she find him, her sweet dear little one?

She searched all over the slope, but Spitzibühl the mountain was totally changed, and could not be recognized as the old Rossberg. Everywhere she looked, the mountain was deeply torn, down to the foundation rocks, wild cliffs and colossal stones. Weeping, she wandered about the ruins till she sank to the ground, dead-tired.

Thus the old Waser and Plazidus had found her. The first was desperately seeking for his sons. All three had been away from home when the catastrophe hit, and mother knew that Lorenz had gone to Spitzibühl.

"Is he here? Is he with you? The Spitzibühl is unharmed. The wandering forests vanished over there," said the old man full of expectation.

"He is not with us," she told him and then related how Lorenz had left to go to her father. "Come, let us both search."

"The cross on the Wildespitz is unharmed," said Plazidus. "We saw it from beneath. Perhaps they are both up there unharmed."

Hope and fellowship gave new strength. The three began the tiresome climb upwards. Finally they got there, and what they found, Berena could only give thanks for. When she now thought about her father, delivered, happy with Jesus, it was nothing but a precious thought.

The men carried him down to Spitzibühl and then Berena went to search further, accompanied by, and under the protection of, the monk.

But where was the child? The child!

As they entered the valley they were appalled by the awful sight that met them. There was devastation, debris and ruin everywhere. Bodies of people and animals lay half buried in rock debris.

Weeping, Berena sought for the child's body. They met other people who were looking for their lost ones; people from the mountain, who had known their relatives in the valley.

The old Waser was found with a look of despair on his face at the filled-up Aa-creek, rolling stones to the side. As the monk and Berena came closer to help, they were stunned. Two children's bodies lay uncovered. The two boys, Ulrich and Matthew, must have suffocated, for their bodies lay there completely unharmed in a hollow, like two fallen rocks.

Ulrich had the remainder of the New Testament in his hand. With all her pain and sorrow, Berena had to rejoice that the two brothers were united in their death. The situation and expression spoke nothing of disunity and separation but only of love and peace.

She pressed a kiss on Ulrich's forehead, then pressed on further. Passing by they saw some men uncovering and digging out a womanly form. A bright blue dress came in view, then shining shoe buckles, a rich blond braid of hair. It was Josepha, the rich girl. She stood in an upright position pressed in by dirt and stones.

Berena turned away from the sight. As she

was turning she saw one of the men pick up from the ground something white, an amulet, the one with the red silk covering. She knew that her father had given it back to the miller's daughter. Now it lay there. It had profited nothing, neither Josepha's father nor his daughter. Both had died a terrible death.

How glad Berena was that she knew that her own beloved father had been saved and blessed by the Saviour.

Many people were standing on the banks of the shore of the Lowerzer Sea. The sea was still boiling and bubbling from the depths because its depths had been so forcefully taken from it. The waves beat together over the ruins of the little chapel on the Schwanau. A lifeless body was swept to the shore.

"The old fisher is dead," sorrowfully said the people that stood around. "He was a good man."

"He was more than that," thought Berena and Plazidus as they looked into his peaceful face. To both of them he had shown the simple way to Jesus.

The waves washed more bodies to the shore, which included people and animals. "This is Alois, the shepherd, and this is the Gisler! We have already pulled ashore the bodies of 30 cows of their herd. Oh, what a stormy wind to have hurled all these through the air! The whole pasture of the Rossberg is come here."

"And the fir forest. See the rows of big fir trees rolling in the waves!"

"Whoa, what is that? That fir is alive! Something is moving on yonder fir tree! Get a boat, a boat!"

With the speed of the wind, they sent a boat to float on the waters, which by now were becoming somewhat calmer.

"A person, it is a person!" called back the young man from the boat. "It is, it's Lorenz Waser!"

Beaming with joy they doubled their efforts. He was their lord and commander, their young friendly lord who all the people on the Schwendi-Alp loved. "He is alive, we will bring him in!"

On the shore a maiden sank to her knees. She had her hands folded and her head bowed in a fervent prayer of thanksgiving.

A new call from the boys in the boat made her look up quickly. "What have we here? Oh look, a cradle, and a smiling child in it! Give the oar here, we will haul it in."

They reached the rocking cradle. Lorenz Waser just then awakened from having been knocked out. The little child from Spitzibühl, bright and happy for again seeing people and because it finally again found his lost milk bottle which had been beside him in the cradle, cooed softly. Having saved two people, the shepherd boys came triumphantly to shore.

Laughing and weeping Berena held her little one in her arms. She could hardly contain so much good fortune after so very heavy sorrowing and heartache. She pressed the child to her heart and covered his small rosy face with kisses. She called him a thousand love names and he repaid everything to her in double measure.

It was a sight that brought tears into the eyes of even the most weather-beaten men. They had laid Lorenz Waser beside her and given him a little drink. Then he was asked to relate what had happened.

"I remember nothing," said he. Then his eyes fastened onto Berena. "Thc only thing I remember is that while I was climbing in the forest above Spitzibühl, suddenly everything became strangely restless. Goats and deer shot past me as if being chased. Great flocks of birds flew over my head with anxious cries in the direction toward Rigi. The tree tops began to roar and to bend, a powerful air pressure slung me to a strong fir tree to which, in my anxiety, I clung with both hands.

"Then there was a horrible, booming, thunderclap and a rolling deafening roar. It was as if the whole Rossberg were in movement. The forest was alive, also my fir tree was with force torn out of the earth. I clung tightly to it and with the air pressure pressing me to it, I was hurled through the air with raging swiftness. My senses left me and when I came to I was swimming in the branches of my fir tree on the foaming waves of the Lowerzer Sea."

Those standing around listened, amazed.

"The mother of God has done another wonder," they said making the sign of the cross. "You must have indeed offered much to her?"

"I had only thought of Jesus," said Lorenz earnestly. "And—and, Berena, Jesus spoke to me."

She smiled at him and said, "I knew well that He had much to tell you. Have you listened to Him right, and also understood?"

For a while he remained silent. Pride and humility fought a short, hard battle. Should he confess in front of this congregated multitude?

Then he sprang up, and standing straight upright, he said, "Listen you people, also you from our Schwendi-Alp. You believed me to have been a good honorable man. It wasn't true. I had thought so myself, and as I couldn't think otherwise I convinced myself and others. I was not good, dear people. I have lived for myself and when something crossed my will I became angry. I have said many cross words to my father and in those horrible minutes of fear and anxiety of death they fell heavy on my heart. I knew that I could not stand before God with them, my sins separated me from Him. I knew from the Book my mother and brothers had, that Jesus desired a different life from me. I knew it also from old Michael Engler, but I didn't want to have anything to do with Jesus. But now I know that without Him I will not become complete. I know that without Him I will be lost, and—and, on the waters of the Lowerzer Sea I have committed myself into His hands. Now my body and life belong to Him."

The longer he talked the more his voice increased in strength and joy. A shine was on his forehead. The men took off their hats and the few women that were there bowed themselves. From the lips of the Capuchin monk came a soft "Amen."

Berena knelt with the child in her arms. Then Lorenz sank to his knees beside her saying, "We want to thank the Lord."

. . . .

High into the clear mountain air had Rigi and Rossberg towered, like shepherds and watchmen of the Golden Meadows. While Rigi slopes mostly gradually toward the valley Rigi-Aa, in soft green meadows, the Rossberg appears to have been torn to its naked rock sides from its peak to its foot.

A mighty wild mountain landslide or avalanche took downward a mass that spread out like a shelf and traversed the valley floor to almost three kilometers.

The little piles of rubble here and there are covered with green and streaked with dark conifer wood or swelled up here and there full of mighty blocks of rock and between them at places gleams a red bedecked pool.

A new Goldau is erected on the wasted, ruined field of the old Goldau. The wild mountain waters of the Rigi-Aa creek were rerouted through the debris of the mountain avalanche.

There is nothing more to fear from the old Rufiberg, the full-of-mischief companion of Rigi. The alpine people live there on the slope and in the valley without fear or anxiety.

In the newly built chapel hangs the old clock of the old covered chapel which had been dug out of the debris of the Aa-creek, to preserve the memory of the disaster to the world. And a painting gives a picture of the former valley of the Golden-Aa *before the mountain moved.*

An old postcard from Switzerland

A view of the valley between the Rufiberg and the Rigi in Switzerland near the Lowerzer narrow valley before the mountain moved. (translated from the above)

Today (see front cover)